Wake up, Henry Rooster!

Text copyright © 2006 by Margriet Ruurs
Illustrations copyright © 2006 by Sean Cassidy

Published in Canada by Fitzhenry & Whiteside,
195 Allstate Parkway, Markham, Ontario L3R 4T8

Published in the United States by Fitzhenry & Whiteside,
311 Washington Street, Brighton, Massachusetts 02135

www.fitzhenry.ca   godwit@fitzhenry.ca

10 9 8 7 6 5 4 3

Library and Archives Canada Cataloguing in Publication
Ruurs, Margriet, 1952-
Wake up, Henry Rooster / Margriet Ruurs ; illustrated by Sean Cassidy.
ISBN 1-55041-952-8
1. Roosters—Juvenile fiction. I. Cassidy, Sean, 1947- II. Title.
PS8585.U97W34 2006   jC813'.54   C2005-907254-7

**U.S. Publisher Cataloging-in-Publication Data
(Library of Congress Standards)**

Ruurs, Margriet, 1952-
Wake up, Henry Rooster / Margriet Ruurs ; illustrated by Sean Cassidy.
[32] p. : col. ill. ; cm.
Summary: Henry loves to stay up late; he's no morning rooster.
But when his father leaves the farm for a convention, it's now
up to Henry to crow the sun up.
ISBN 1-55041-952-8
1. Roosters— Fiction — Juvenile literature. I. Cassidy, Sean, 1947- I. Title.
[E] dc22   PZ7.R945Wa   2006

Fitzhenry & Whiteside acknowledges with thanks the Canada Council for the Arts,
and the Ontario Arts Council for their support of our publishing program.
We acknowledge the financial support of the Government of Canada through the
Book Publishing Industry Development Program (BPIDP) for our publishing activities.

Design by Wycliffe Smith Design Inc.

Printed in Hong Kong

Wake up, Henry Rooster!

By Margriet Ruurs

Illustrated by Sean Cassidy

Fitzhenry & Whiteside

For Harrison, Victoria, Jessica, and Garrett,
who always get up at the crack of dawn.
                                        —Margriet

For Mum.
Thanks for waking me all those mornings.
                                        —Sean

When he was a baby rooster, Henry loved to sleep in. During the night he screamed and hollered like a skinny pig. But in the morning, when all the farm awoke, Baby Henry slept, as quiet as a lamb.

Even when he was older, Henry loved to sleep in.

Henry's father worried about his son. "He stays up too late," he complained. "Then he won't get up all day. That boy's lazy!"

"He's not lazy," Henry's mother protested. "He puts in the same hours. Henry's just not a morning rooster."

His aunties, Henny and Penny, cackled at Henry. "Comb your comb. Sit up straight."

His older sisters, Little and Red, nagged him. "Clean your coop. It looks like the pigsty."

Henry was tired of everyone telling him what to do. He loved staying up late. He liked his coop the way it was.

Henry just wanted to have fun.

One day Henry's father packed his bag to go to the Roosters' Union Convention. He shook Henry awake.

"Son," he said, "as the oldest boy, you will have to do my work while I'm away this week. It will be up to you to crow the farm awake at the crack of dawn."

And with that, his father tied a bandana around his neck, pecked Henry's mother on the cheek, and was off.

That night, Henry played cards with the goats and popped corn with the pigs. When he finally rolled into bed, it was very late, indeed.

In no time at all, Henry's mother was shaking him awake. "Henry," she clucked. "Time to do your job. Get up on the roof."

Henry dragged himself up to the barn roof. Then he stretched and croaked, "Cock-a(yawn)-doodle-do."

Slowly the sun rose and woke the animals and people on the farm for a hard day's work.

Henry stumbled back to bed.

The next night, Henry
played with the sheep
and danced with the
cows. When he finally
stumbled into bed, it was very, *very* late,
indeed.

Soon, much too soon, his mother was shaking him awake.

"Henry!" she cluck-clucked. "Time to do your job! Make the sun rise or we won't get any work done!" Then she shoved Henry out of the coop.

Too tired to climb to the roof, Henry dragged himself onto the fence. He stretched and croaked, "Cock-a(yawn)-doodle(yawn)-do."

It took some doing that morning, but eventually the sun rose and woke the animals and people on the farm for a hard day's work.

Henry stumbled back to bed.

The night after that, Henry horsed around in the barn. When he finally crawled into bed, he read for a long time before falling asleep. It was very, very, *very* late, indeed.

He had only been asleep for a little while when his mother shook him awake.

"*Henry!*" she cluck-cluck-clucked. "I slept in this morning! You're very, very, *very* late! Go wake up the sun or we'll all be in trouble!"

With stiff legs, Henry clambered up onto the barn roof and shook his sleepy head. He croaked, "Cock-a(yawn)-(yawn)doodle-(yawn)do."

The sun was late that day. The farmer didn't milk the cows on time, and the farmer's wife didn't collect the eggs before breakfast.

"*Henry*. The farm depends on you!" his mother scolded.

"*Henry*. You shouldn't dilly-dally so!" his aunties complained.

"*Henry*. You should shape up!" his sisters cackled.

But Henry couldn't rise early. He just wasn't a morning rooster.

The week was a disaster. The sun frowned at him all day from behind dark clouds.

None of the animals were fed on time. The farmer was late delivering his crop to the train station. The farmer's wife slept through an important garden club meeting. And the farmer's children missed the school bus.

They all blamed Henry.

Henry tried to talk his mother into waking everybody up.
But she wouldn't be bribed.

"Hens don't crow," she said. "Besides, I do a full day's work
laying eggs, looking after the chicks, pecking up after
everybody. Waking up the farm is your job."

Henry tried to talk his sisters into doing his job.
But they just laughed at him.

He tried to convince his friend Betsy to moo
the farm awake. But she shook her head.

"Cows don't climb onto roofs,"
she said. "Besides, no one
would hear my moo."

Finally, Henry asked the wise old goat for advice.

The goat stroked his beard and stared at Henry. He hummed softly to himself.

The goat said, in a mysterious voice, "You can't get up early…yet you seem to be very good at staying up late. Just how late do you think you can stay up?" And then he dismissed Henry with a wave of his hoof.

Henry thought about what the old goat had asked him. "Hmmm…perhaps I could stay up even later…."

Then Henry had an idea!

The very next night, Henry partied with the pigs.
He sang with the sheep.
He tap-danced with the turkeys.
He finished reading his book.
He listened to his favorite moo-sic.
He stayed up later than ever before, and,
just before he fell asleep…

…Henry climbed up onto the barn roof.

"Cock-a-doodle-doo!" He crowed with all his might.

"*Cock-a-doodle-do!*" He shook his comb happily and crowed some more.

"COCK-A-DOODLE-DO!" He crowed so loud that he scared the moon away. It slid behind a cloud and didn't show its face for a long time.

"*COCK-A-DOODLE-DO!*" Henry crowed until the sun peeked over the horizon to see what was going on.

Then the sun painted the sky pink and woke up the animals and people on the farm for a hard day's work.

All except Henry.
Henry slept the day away.